THE ODD SQUAD

KING KARL

MICHAEL FRY

ff

FABER & FABER

First published in the USA by Disney · Hyperion Books,
an imprint of Disney Book Group LLC, in 2013

First published in the UK in 2014
by Faber & Faber Limited
Bloomsbury House,
74–77 Great Russell Street,
London WC1B 3DA

Printed in the UK by CPI Group (UK) Ltd, Croydon CR0 4YY

Text and illustrations copyright © 2013 by Michael Fry

The right of Michael Fry to be identified as author
of this work has been asserted in accordance with Section 77
of the Copyright, Designs and Patents Act 1988

A CIP record for this book
is available from the British Library

ISBN 978–0–571–31441–6

1 3 5 7 9 10 8 6 4 2

TO MUM:
WHO NEVER SAID,
'CUT YOUR HAIR AND
GET A REAL JOB.'

NICK, MOLLY and **KARL** are
The Odd Squad!

ROY is a mutant troll bully.

BECKY is Nick's
girlfriend (in an alternate
universe).

Nick lives with his **MUM, MEMAW** (that's his grandmother) and his dog **JANICE**.

Then there's

MR DUPREE the school janitor

and

DR DANIELS the school counsellor,

and a couple of other kids at school: **SIMONE**

and **ALICE**...

Those are the important guys, there are plenty more in the book . . .

NOTE FROM NICK ON FOOD

Hello to all my UK readers!
I'm told you don't have Jell-O Meat or
Tater Tots at school over there.
On the one hand you're lucky. On the
other, you are super *un*lucky.
Jell-O Meat is the grossest thing on
the planet. I mean, it's DISGUSTING. It's
kind of like corned beef in a meat jelly.
Yeah, I know.
Tater Tots, however . . . they're crunchy
little mounds of potato-ey goodness.
Mmmm.
Oh, and Hot Dots are awesome candy
(which you call sweets)!

CHAPTER 1

'That's stupid,' Molly said into my earpiece. 'They should be called Robosquids.'

'They're Squidbots!' I said. 'Because that's what they're called in *NanoNerd #83*: 'Time Waits for No Squid'. Now, do you want to play or not?'

'I *want* to find out what Karl is up to, but he's taking a nap, and this is only slightly less boring. So we just blast the Robosquids?'

NO! SET YOUR NANOBLASTER TO STUN! IF YOU KILL THEM, THEY JUST MULTIPLY.

STUN? EVERYBODY SAYS STUN. I LIKE CHILL.

GALAXY FLEET CADET CAP. *

*UNDERWEAR

NanoNerd: Squidpocalypse is a simple online game. All you have to do is blast squidbots before they blast you. I play with people from all over the world.

And Molly.

'I told you this was a stupid game,' said Molly.

Molly's a friend. Sort of. We're both in Safety Patrol with Karl at Emily Dickinson Middle School (EMDS for short). It should be called the Freak Patrol.

Our guidance counsellor, Dr Daniels, made us all join Safety Patrol because she said we had 'peer allergies' and needed to fit in. At first, we thought it was lame. We did stuff like try to make sure sixth-graders didn't drown in the water fountains.

But it got better. We helped some kids and actually became sort of heroes for a few weeks. Now it's pretty cool. Well, not that cool. Okay, it's still pretty lame. But we do get out of lessons a lot.

And there's the snacks.

The beret Karl wears has a nannycam that broadcasts to a private website. We call it the Beret-Cam. He started out wearing it for undercover Safety

Patrol stuff, but now he wears it all the time. Molly and I watch the feed on my phone. That's how we learned Karl got an invitation to join MLEZ.

MLEZ used to be Emily (they sound the same). Emily is this made-up thing kids at EDMS have used for years to explain the mysteries of middle school.

Like it's the ghost of Emily Dickinson, or something. But it's not.

Emily became real when it became MLEZ: the name on Karl's invitation. That's when we figured out that MLEZ was Emily, and she or he or it had been secretly helping Safety Patrol behind the scenes.

Like the time I was helping this bully Roy (now retired) get his stuffed pig back after MLEZ released a pet python named Willy that stampeded the Science Fair.

MLEZ did stuff that was so crazy, it was like it controlled the school. And now MLEZ wants Karl. Seriously, Karl? I don't even want to think about what he'd do if he were part of some group that ran the school.

C'MON, YOU KNOW YOU WANT ONE!

DAILY KARL HUG

It's all pretty strange. But Molly and I will figure it out. It's like Memaw says: 'A walrus riding a bike is weird until you find out his monster truck is at the garage.'

'See if Karl's awake yet?' asked Molly into my earpiece.

I checked the Beret-Cam.

'Yeah, he's dressing up Stanley as Abe Lincoln.' (Stanley is Karl's pet parakeet.)

'Of course he is,' said Molly.

'Nick?'

I turned around to see Mum and Memaw standing at my door. I whispered to Molly, 'I gotta go.'

'He's stretching them out,' said Memaw. 'And we just bought them!'

'It's those comic books and video games,' said Memaw. 'He thinks he's NanoSnot.'

'NanoNerd!' I said. 'His suit is called a Nano*Bot*.'

'NanoSnot was born without a spleen,' said Memaw.

'Nick! Stop yelling at your grandmother,' said Mum.

Memaw turned to Mum. 'If you ask me, the child's hopped up on the glue guns.'

Mum eyed Memaw. 'Glue guns?'

Memaw continued, 'You know, from all the NanoTots he eats.'

'NanoPops,' I said.

'Oh, you mean *glutens*,' said Mum.

'That too,' said Memaw.

First, I eat only two and a half boxes of NanoPops per week and second, I don't have a problem with gluten. I'm not like Oscar Hernandez at school who can eat only three things.

Lucky guy.

'Nick, is everything okay?' asked Mum.

'I'm fine!' I said.

Memaw said, 'He's getting to *that* age.'

'What age?' asked Mum.

'The too-old-to-go-underwear-shopping-with-his-grandmother age.'

'Mother, he's growing up.' Mum turned to me. 'Now, honey, I don't care if you play NanoJock, but let's give your underwear a break.'

I slid the underwear off my head. 'Fine,' I said.

'Remember,' said Mum, 'if you ever need to talk, I'm here.'

'Okay,' I said.

'Love you,' said Mum.

I LOVE YOU TOO.

WHEN I'M GONE, HE'S GOING TO MISS THE TIME WE SPENT IN THE BOYS SHORT-AND-SLIM SECTION.

CHAPTER 2

The next day before school Molly and I watched Karl from down the hall.

I said, 'What I want to know is where did Karl find an Abe Lincoln hat that tiny?'

'This is Karl we're talking about, right?' Molly replied.

KARL'S LOCKER

CEILING FAN   FLOSS

BOLD SPICE →

EMERGENCY TUNA →

MUM →

SPARE UNDER-WEAR →

← MIRROR

TUNA TUNA

Molly shook her head. 'I can't believe MLEZ wants Karl, but they don't want us.'

'Or at least me,' I said. 'I mean, I believed in MLEZ before *anyone* did.'

Molly glared at me. 'It's not a competition.'

'Of course it isn't. They want Karl!'

Molly sighed. 'Eventually Karl will lead us to MLEZ.'

'I don't know. We've been following him for two weeks.' When he's not in the bathroom . . .

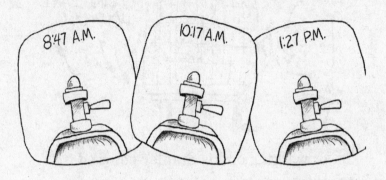

. . . or reading to his sea monkeys . . .

. . . or teaching Stanley the Gettysburg Address . . .

. . . or working on his Stanley-powered toothbrush for the annual Schoolseum (where classrooms become minimuseums).

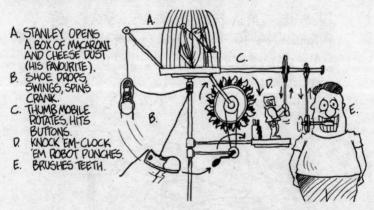

'Check on the Beret-Cam one last time before the bell rings,' said Molly.

I pulled out my phone just as . . .

It was Mr Wickler, my maths teacher. 'You know the rules,' he said. 'No operating mobile devices during school hours.'

'But class hasn't start—'

CHAPTER 3

I'm a maths ninja. One second there's a problem. The next second . . .

. . . there's an answer.

I didn't used to be good at maths, but then one day everything clicked and I knew the answers—*without* showing my work. Not because I was hiding my work. Just because there was no work to show.

It's weird, but I always get the right answer. And somehow I can even help other kids get the right answers. It's always been cool with everyone. Everyone except Mr Wickler: the worst teacher in school.

There are only a few really bad teachers at Emily Dickinson Middle School.

But the worst by far is Wickler.

'X equals two,' I said without getting up.

Mr Wickler shook his head. 'That is not the complete answer, Mr Ramsey.'

'It's the only answer there is,' I said.

The right answer is never enough for him. He has to make me go to the board and show the work I don't need to show.

'Once again, Mr Ramsey declines to show us his work,' said Mr Wickler. 'As I've informed him many times, maths is not about the destination. It's about the . . .

That makes zero sense. Why take seventeen thousand light years from Earth to Oomzotz VII when you can use a wormhole?

'I'll show you my work,' I said as I got up and walked to the board.

'Mr Ramsey dares to fight against the tide!' said Mr Wickler. 'And for that, he will be rewarded!'

Mr Wickler wrote out a hall pass to Dr Daniels's office and handed it to me.

CHAPTER 4

I've made the *journey* to Dr Daniels's office lots of times. It's a long way. And I make it longer every time I do it.

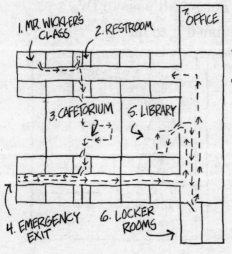

1. EXIT OLD-WORMS-FOR-BRAINS' CLASS.
2. MAKE ZOMBIE FACES IN THE MIRROR.
3. SWEET-TALK THE LUNCH LADIES OUT OF THREE TATER TOTS.
4. CONSIDER MAKING A RUN FOR IT. REALIZE MY LEGS ARE TOO SHORT.
5. LOOK UP "FART" IN THE BIG DICTIONARY.
6. ENTER, THEN EXIT WHEN REPELLED BY CLOUD OF TOXIC BODY SPRAY.
7. AVOID AT ALL COSTS!

As I looked for more places to stall, I rounded a corner and ran into Mr Dupree.

He smiled. 'Journey's end, I see.'

Mr Dupree is the school janitor, Safety Patrol advisor, and all around weird hippie dude.

I said, 'How did you know . . . '

Mr Dupree likes to quote this guy Shakespeare who lived, like, a million years ago and sort of spoke English, but not really. He does it mostly to confuse and annoy everyone.

'Whatever,' I said.

'Mr Wickler again?'

I shrugged.

'Still not showing your work?'

I shrugged again.

'As long as you get the right answer, what difference does it make, right?'

I said, 'That's what I thought!'

'Nick, you and I are a lot alike.'

Groan. I knew exactly what was coming next.

'Did I ever tell you about the time I was a roller-coaster test rider?' asked Mr Dupree.

Double groan.

He continued. 'I tested all the big coasters . . .

THE KNOTERATOR

THE DOUBLE HELIX OF DOOM

THE SKULL DUSTER

'One day I was testing the new Stomach Pumper at Land-O-Screams. The Stomach Pumper was the biggest and fastest coaster of its day.

'My first ride went fine except for one thing.

'A coaster splash should be big, but not too big. It should soak the riders, not drown them. I told the engineer he needed to lower the splash-approach angle.

'He disagreed. He thought the splash angle should be *raised*. He showed me his calculations. When I wouldn't budge, he said, "If you're so certain, show me your work!"

'But I couldn't. I wasn't an engineer. I just knew from experience.

'Then, against my advice, he raised the angle. He said, "You want to see my work? Watch."

'He tested the coaster himself. And we all got to see his work.'

Like most of Mr Dupree's stories, this one made zero sense. I started to make my that's-so-lame face when Dr Daniels walked up.

She looked at the hall pass in my hand. 'Not again, Nick.'

That's what she said. What she meant was:

WHAT HAVE I DONE NOW? DO YOU HAVE IT IN FOR ME? IF YOU SHRUG ONE MORE TIME, I'M GOING TO SCREAM.

I shrugged.

She didn't scream. But I could tell she wanted to.

Instead she sighed and said, 'Come with me.'

'I'll see you tonight, Nick,' said Mr Dupree. 'Maxine and I have tango practice.'

Triple groan.

Mr Dupree and Memaw are dating. Which is gross.

And weird. And shows ZERO consideration for my needs.

NICK'S NEEDS
1. NOT BE GROSSED OUT.
2. NOT FEEL WEIRD.
3. NOT BE EMBARRASSED.
4. DONUTS. WHENEVER I WANT THEM.

'Nick! I'm waiting,' whisper-shouted Dr Daniels.

Mr Dupree said, 'Now, what did I do with Doris?'

As I ran after Dr Daniels, I thought, In how many different ways can things NOT go my way?

I CAN'T COUNT THAT HIGH.

REALLY NOT HELPING!

CHAPTER 5

The good thing about being sent to Dr Daniels's
office is that she's always got some new therapy
doll or lame brochures to entertain me.

The bad thing about being sent to Dr Daniels's
office is that she always wants to fix what isn't
broken.

'Nick, we've worked through your problems
with being bullied by Roy.

SHOVE!

ROY

ROY SHOVED ME INTO MY LOCKER SO DR. DANIELS PUT ME IN SAFETY PATROL WHERE WE DECIDED TO GET EVEN WITH ROY AND STEAL HIS SECRET STUFFED PIG, WHICH MADE ME A BULLY TOO. SO I HELPED ROY GET IT BACK FROM A PYTHON BY RUINING THE SCIENCE FAIR. →

IT'S TRUE!

'And we overcame your issues with bullying yourself.

I BULLIED MYSELF TO FLUSH OUT MLEZ. ONLY TO BRING ZERO TOLERANCE DOWN ON THE SCHOOL AND ALMOST GET MYSELF SUSPENDED WHEN I WAS FRAMED BY A FAKE FRENCH GIRL FOR BULLYING.

NO, REALLY!

'And now we're going to get to the bottom of your problems with Mr Wickler.'

The problem with getting to the bottom of my problems with Mr Wickler is that there is no bottom to my problems with Mr Wickler.

MY PROBLEMS WITH MR WICKLER

1. HE HATES ME.
2. HE WANTS ME TO FAIL.
3. HE MAY BE AN ALIEN.
4. I'M PRETTY SURE WORMS CONTROL HIS BRAIN.
5. HE SMELLS LIKE OLD SOCKS.
6. I'VE NEVER SEEN HIM BLINK.
   SNACKS ON PENCIL SHAVINGS.

But I didn't say all that. I just said, 'Good luck.'

'Nick, you're the best in your class at maths. You solve the problems in your head so well, you don't need to show your work.'

'What's wrong with that?'

'Nothing. But . . . '

'But what?'

'But on the BASS test, you *have* to show your work.'

Quadruple groan! BASS stands for Basic Assessment of Student Skills. I say it stands for Big Attack on Student Smarts. The whole universe stops for eight weeks before the test while all the teachers teach the tests. Nothing normal like class discussion, or cool stuff like blowing things up in science class. Nope, just drill, drill, drill on sample test questions like:

8. If Judy has \$1.75 and apples are 25¢ each, how many apples can she buy?

Who cares? SHE'S BUYING FRUIT!

'Nick, we need you to do your very best on the BASS test so we can get an exemplary rating. You know what happens if we get an exemplary rating?'

I shrugged.

'We get more resources for the school and a concert right here in the cafetorium by none other than . . .

Boy Toyz is this lame boy band. Not my thing. They're not all that different from Brobot Rebellion or DudeFarm.

'Last year we were only five points short of exemplary. If just a handful of students like you live up to their potential, your scores could make the difference.'

Great. If it got out that I didn't do all I could to help make Boy Toyz happen, every girl in this school would hate me forever. Even Becky, my alternate-universe girlfriend and this-universe regular friend, would zap me into dust with her Hate Ray.

All girls have them, you know.

Dr Daniels did her best impression of a scary cheerleader. 'You can do it, Nick! I know it! All you have to do is show your work!'

The bell rang as I left Dr Daniels's office. Students streamed into the halls while I leaned against the wall and stared at my shoes. How can I show my work when I don't have any work to show?

I needed help.

LOUDER!

PLEASE, GLORIOUS EXALTED SUPREME BEING OF IMMENSE MATHS SKILLS, WILL YOU PLEASE HELP ME SHOW MY WORK?

No way.

'Karl got a text.'

I looked up. It was Molly. She was smiling.

'From MLEZ?' I asked. 'Wait. How can you see Karl's texts? Only my phone gets his Beret-Cam feed, and Mr Wickler took my phone away.'

'Karl sits in front of me in English. He was at the board doing a book report when his phone buzzed.'

'How do you know it was MLEZ?'

'Who else would be texting him? He only gets texts from us and his mum, and she would never let him go to Rocket Park.'

Rocket Park is this old park near the school that the city hasn't got around to fun-proofing yet.

The swings are so tall, you need a parachute to land safely.

The super-long seesaw could send you flying
into Earth's orbit.

Best of all, it has one of
those really tall rocket ships
with lots of rusty sharp edges
for climbing and sliding. It's
totally dangerous.

And *totally* awesome.

Except for one thing.

'But what about Arnold?' I
said.

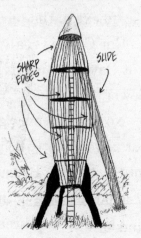

Molly stared at me. 'Seriously?'

According to school legend, guarding this playground/minefield is the scariest, nastiest, foulest creature on Earth.

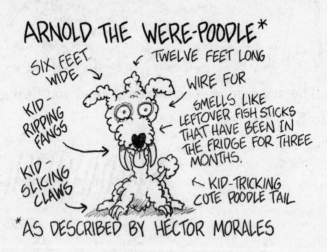

ARNOLD THE WERE-POODLE*

SIX FEET WIDE

TWELVE FEET LONG

WIRE FUR

KID-RIPPING FANGS

SMELLS LIKE LEFTOVER FISH STICKS THAT HAVE BEEN IN THE FRIDGE FOR THREE MONTHS.

KID-SLICING CLAWS

KID-TRICKING CUTE POODLE TAIL

*AS DESCRIBED BY HECTOR MORALES

Hector Morales was the only one who had ever seen Arnold. He said he saw him come out of Rat Cave next to the park.

Rat Cave is really a storm sewer. We call it Rat Cave because it sounds better than Rat Storm Sewer.

No one has ever gone into Rat Cave and come out alive. Mostly because no one has ever gone into Rat Cave. Because . . . hello? It's full of rats!

'You're going with me, right?' said Molly.

I took a deep breath. 'I guess.'

Yeah, I'll go. Hector could be exaggerating. Except for those times he claimed his brother was his clone and that cat spit cures warts, he's *totally* reliable.

CHAPTER 7

When school finished, I got my phone from Mr Wickler (and a lecture on dinosaur times) . . .

WHEN I WAS YOUR AGE, WE DIDN'T HAVE FANCY SMARTPHONES. WHEN WE NEEDED TO COMMUNICATE, WE USED SMOKE SIGNALS OR YELLED REALLY LOUD.

WHATEVER.

Weirdo.

Afterwards I headed straight for Rocket Park to meet Molly. When I got there, I found Molly, but there was no sign of Karl – just some little kid and his mum playing on the swings.

We hid behind some bushes and waited.

I said, 'You see Arnold?'

Molly shook her head. 'There is no Arnold.'

'Just like you used to say there was no Emily. You don't know anything.'

Molly glared at me. 'Like you know anything.'

'I know a lot. I know you're annoying and I know I don't want to be here and I *absolutely* know if I cut myself on a sharp edge, my mum is going to kill me.'

'If Arnold doesn't get you first,' Molly said.

'Shut up.'

'You shut up.'

'What is that?' asked Molly.

'It's Karl,' I said. 'Covered in bubble wrap?'

Karl headed for the rocket slide. On his way he

spotted the mum and her son.

Karl said, 'You haven't seen a kid-snacking were-poodle, have you?'

The mum shook her head.

'Good.' Karl smiled at the little boy. 'Next time, bubble wrap.'

Karl disappeared into the rocket slide.

'Check the Beret-Cam,' said Molly.

The Beret-Cam was dark. 'I can't see anything through the bubble wrap,' I said.

Molly started tiptoeing toward the rocket. 'MLEZ must be waiting at the top of the rocket. Let's go.'

I really wanted to follow her, but there was the Arnold situation and . . .

Molly rolled her eyes, slipped her backpack off

38

her shoulders, and handed it me.

'What?' I said.

'Put it on frontways.'

Yeah, I looked stupid. But it was a protection-from-sharp-edges-and-wrath-of-Mum kind of stupid.

As we snuck up to the rocket, I noticed the little boy and his mum staring at us. I pointed to the rocket. 'He's right. Next time, bubble wrap.'

Molly and I approached the rocket. It was dark and creepy, and I swear it really did smell like three-month-old fish sticks.

Inside, there were three levels, connected by a single ladder.

'I'll go first,' whispered Molly.

I whispered back, 'No, I'll go first. You left the bush first.'

'What difference does it make?'

'You can't go first twice!'

'Fine. Go first.'

Great. I didn't really want to go first, but if Molly went first twice, it'd be like she was in charge when we're really both in charge, even though she always acts like she's in charge.

I started to climb the ladder. As I poked my head into the first level, the frontpack got stuck.

I yanked. Nothing. I yanked harder.

'Ow!' I hissed as the strap dug into my shoulder.

Molly said, 'Sharp edge?'

'Shh, I'm fine.'

I yanked again.

The strap dug deeper and then . . .

Molly rolled her eyes. 'I knew I should have gone first.'

'Shut up and help me.'

As Molly reached up to adjust the frontpack, we heard Karl above us say, 'You waited for me! I knew you would. Are you okay? You look okay. What? Me? I'm fine.'

I looked at Molly. 'Who's he talking to?'

'MLEZ?' whispered Molly.

Karl continued, 'You like it here, don't you? It's your favourite place. I like it too. Except, you know, for the sharp edges and the killer poodle.'

Molly started to climb to the third level when . . .

WHAT DO YOU NEED FROM ME? I'LL DO ANYTHING TO KEEP YOU SAFE!

Whatever was going on sounded weird, and Karl is plenty weird enough without extra MLEZ weirdness. We started climbing faster.

Karl said, 'I'm ready. Just tell me what to do.'

'Karl! No!' I yelled as I scrambled up the

ladder after Molly.

That's when I saw my worst nightmare come to life.

What happened next involved a lot of screaming and a lot of popping.

Followed by more popping, then sliding, and

ending with way too much unintentional hugging.

After we untangled ourselves and scooted back

a few feet, Molly said to Karl, 'You were talking to Stanley the whole time?'

'He flew away from home,' said Karl. 'He always flies to the rocket. I think he likes to perch on top and pretend he's a space parakeet. What are you doing here?'

Molly and I exchanged looks.

'Um . . . we . . . you know . . . we always come here,' I said.

'Yeah, always,' said Molly.

I said, 'It's . . . um . . . fun.'

Karl smiled. 'I know what's going on. You like each other.'

I looked at Molly. Molly looked at me.

'No!' we cried.

'It makes sense. You're always together. You pretend to be mean to each other.' Karl pointed at Molly's backpack. 'And you're carrying her backpack.'

I dropped Molly's frontpack as if it were on fire.

Molly glared at me. 'Thanks.'

Arnold started licking my hand. I pushed him away. He looked hurt. I gave up. He kept licking.

We may not have figured out who MLEZ is, but

I know I learned one very important lesson.

CHAPTER 8

After the park incident, Molly came over to my house so we could figure out what to do next.

She said, 'Okay, so what do we know about MLEZ?"

I said, 'MLEZ is super-secret and super-smart. He or she or it knows the school . . . I don't know . . . It's like it's invisible?'

'So it has to be somebody at school.'

'But who? There are hundreds of kids and a bunch of teachers and staff. We can't follow them all around.'

Molly said, 'But we can look at them all in one place.'

'How?'

'The yearbook! We check everybody. Eliminate them one by one. *Somebody* has to make sense.'

So that's what we did.

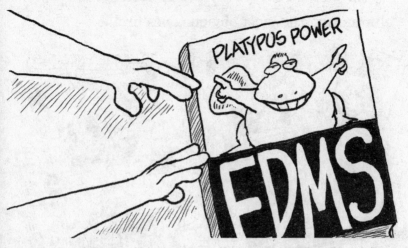

Page by page.

We checked everybody. We started by eliminating the most obvious ones first.

Then we eliminated the teachers and staff, including Dr Daniels and Mr Dupree.

By the end, we were right back where we started. Before we could figure out our next move, we were interrupted by music from downstairs.

'What is that?' asked Molly.

I rolled my eyes. 'You don't want to know.'

Molly went out into the hall to look before I could stop her.

PRACTISING THE TANGO

Molly said, 'I better go.'

'I'll clear a path,' I said.

After Molly left, I wondered why adults were always embarrassing me. Is it something I do? Something I say? Am I giving off some sort of telepathic embarrass-me signal?

NICK'S THOUGHTS

MIND MELD

DONUTS

SPRINKLES

NO.

CHAPTER 9

I tried to escape back to my room, as Mr Dupree twirled Memaw into my path.

'Nick! You're just in time to see our big finish,' said Memaw.

'I can't wait,' I lied.

Mr Dupree said, 'Your grandmother is an excellent dancer.'

'Your lead, sir, is divine!' said Memaw.

No, it wasn't enough just to regular-embarrass me, they had to *epically* embarrass me.

'You're doing everything I'm doing except backwards and in orthopaedic shoes!' said Mr Dupree.

Everyone knows the only way to relieve epic embarrassment is to . . .

Memaw said, 'Ready . . . two . . . three . . . dip!'

'Wait! No!' yelled Mr Dupree.

You know how time slows down when your mum screams when she sees you cooking hot dogs in the dishwasher?

What happened next was a lot like that.

THUNK!

'My butt!' yelled Memaw. 'I BROKE MY BUTT!'
Mum would later correct her. Memaw actually fractured her coccyx. But a broken coccyx doesn't really draw a crowd.

As Memaw moaned on the floor and Mr Dupree groaned on the couch, I called 999. Then I called Mum. She arrived at the same time as the paramedics and went into full nurse mode.

It's a lot like her yelling-at-me mode.

We all ended up in A & E, which you'd think would be cool, but it isn't because my mum works there and everyone has to lie to me about how much I've grown and ask stupid questions like, 'Do you have a girlfriend?'

Eventually I did what all kids do when they want to be left alone. I buried my head in my mobile phone and checked Karl's Beret-Cam.

Whoa! They're meeting at Outdoor Temporary Class #7? No one uses that room except for . . . I texted Molly.

Nick: MLEZ to meet Karl after
school tomorrow
Molly: Where?
Nick: OTC #7
Molly: Chess Club?

Chess Club is the lamest club in school. I know I said Saftey Patrol is the lamest, but when I said that, I'd forgotten about Chess Club. Which is easy to do because anyone who joins Chess Club just sort of stops reflecting light.

'Nick?

Mum stood in front of me. 'Why are you rubbing your shoulder?

I didn't know I was rubbing my shoulder.

She pulled my shirt aside to reveal a bright bruise.

'Oh, that,' I said. 'It's just from my backpack.'

'Your backpack?'

I couldn't tell her I'd been at Rocket Park. I was already in enough trouble. I said, 'I guess it's . . . um . . . you know . . . heavy?'

'You think?'

Uh-oh. Here it comes. The my-son-is-turning-into-a-stooped-troll-because-he-carries-around-a-sixteen-ton-backpack lecture.

But that didn't happen. Instead she said, 'We'll deal with that later. Right now I need to talk to you about Memaw.'

55

'Memaw's going to be in a wheelchair, and I'm going to have to change my schedule to take care of her while you're at school. I'm going to need you to come straight home and take over when I go to work.'

'Wait. I can't. I . . . '

'You have to.'

That's when Mr Dupree and Memaw wheeled up. They were feeling no pain.

Unlike me.

CHAPTER 10

'A helper what?' I said.

'A helper monkey!' said Karl as we walked to the Safety Patrol meeting.

'You're making this up,' I said.

'No! They help people who've been hurt,' said Karl. 'They reach for stuff, open jars, find the remote . . . all sorts of things.'

'I can do all that for Memaw,' I said. 'She doesn't need a monkey.'

'But if she had a monkey, then you wouldn't have to rush home. You could do other stuff.'

I stopped. Did Karl know Molly and I had been following him? I looked at Karl. 'What other stuff?'

'I don't know. Like come over to my house and play Old Maid with my sea monkeys. Even though they cheat.'

Whew. Karl was just being Karl. Which made me wonder again what MLEZ wanted with him.

Karl said, 'I can get Memaw a helper monkey.'

'What? How?'

'My mum's a volunteer at the Monkey See and Do Centre where they train them.'

'You're kidding?'

Karl looked confused. 'I'd never kid about a thing like that.'

'I'll get back to you,' I said as we arrived at the meeting.

Becky, my alternate-universe girlfriend, and Simone, the former fake French kid, had joined Safety Patrol. I'm not sure why. Probably for the snacks.

'Who called this meeting?' I asked.

'I did,' said Mr Dupree behind us.

'Just before he dropped my grandma and broke her butt,' I added.

Karl said, 'Grandmas have very delicate butts. You have to handle them with care. Wait. That didn't come out right.'

'Forget about my back and her butt. Doris is missing.'

'Doris Florbt?' said Karl. 'I just saw her in the hall. She's always looking at me weird.'

'She has a lazy eye,' said Becky. 'She looks at everyone weird.'

Karl said, 'Oh. So it's not me, then?'

No one said anything.

'No, Karl, it's not you!' said Mr Dupree. 'And it's not Doris Florbt. It's Doris the Plunger. And she's missing.'

'A plunger?' I said.

Mr Dupree nodded. 'A very special plunger. In fact, the very first plunger: #001.'

Karl was no longer the weirdest person in the room.

'Doris cannot be lost on my watch,' said Mr Dupree.

I said, 'Um . . . it's just a plunger.'

'Nick, have you ever lost something special someone gave you?' asked Mr Dupree.

'Yeah. I lost my grandfather's watch.'

'Did you say, "It's just a watch"?'

'No.'

'Why not?'

'The watch was special.'

'Why?'

'Because Memaw gave it to me.'

'Watches and plungers don't have value. People have value. Spotless Bo gave me Doris. If I lose Doris, it's like . . .'

'Losing Spotless Bo?'

'Right,' said Mr. Dupree as he turned to the others. 'Now, I want everyone to keep their eyes open and help me find Doris.'

Karl stared at Mr Dupree.

'You can blink, Karl,' said Mr Dupree.

Karl blinked. 'Oh, good. Once during a staring contest with Stanley, my eyelids got so dry, my mum had to spit in them so they'd close.'

'Eww . . .' we all groaned. And just like that, Karl regained the lead in the Weird Olympics.

CHAPTER 11

As much as we wanted to help Mr Dupree, Molly and I had a bigger problem: how to tail Karl to his big meeting with MLEZ.

I came up with a plan. It was a great plan. Way better than all my old plans that only looked like great plans. This plan not only looked like a great plan, but it had that great-plan smell.

NICK'S ABSOLUTELY GUARANTEED TO WORK OR YOUR MONEY BACK. PLAN

STEP 1
MOLLY STAYS AT SCHOOL.
I GO HOME TO MEMAW.

STEP 2
I MONITOR KARL ON THE BERET-CAM.
MOLLY TAILS KARL.

MOLLY AND I STAY IN TOUCH BY PHONE.

And the plan worked perfectly . . . right up until Step 1.

After the ten minutes it took to go through the list (Rub her neck? Again?), I started cooking a box of mac 'n' cheese on the stove.

My phone rang. It was Molly. 'What's happening?' I said.

'I'm waiting for Shy Bladder Boy.'

'Nick!' yelled Memaw. 'I'm fading!'

'Coming!' I yelled as I turned up the heat under the saucepan.

'Wait. Here he is,' said Molly.

'Stay close,' I said, watching on the Beret-Cam as Karl left the bathroom. 'I need you to report what you hear.'

Memaw yelled, 'Nick! I can't find the remote!'

Groan. I knew exactly where it was. It's where it always is. . . .

SOMEONE STOLE IT!

REMOTE

'Hang on. I'll be right back,' I whispered to Molly.

I ran to Memaw, pointed to the remote, and listened not-too-patiently to how *she* didn't put it in her hair, then ran back to the kitchen.

WHAT HAPPENED?

'Karl's gone!' cried Molly. 'I followed him outside. He was heading for OTC #7 when my ponytail hit a branch and got caught in a spiderweb.'

I made a mental note: next time, no freakishly tall partners.

Molly continued, 'After I got my hair loose, I looked up and he was gone.'

I said, 'He must be in the OTC #7, but I can't see a thing on my end.'

Molly said, 'I can't see anything, either. The blinds are drawn on the windows.'

'Can you hear anything?'

'Hang on.'

And that's when I saw something seriously weird on the Beret-Cam.

Was that an Emily Dickinson mask?

The only reason I knew it was Emily Dickinson is because the school's named after her and there's a big creepy painting of her next to the office. It's creepy because her eyes follow you everywhere!

I had no idea who was behind the mask.

'Nick!' yelled Memaw. 'I'm going into shock!'

I seriously doubted that. 'Just a sec!' I yelled.

Molly hissed, 'Quiet! Someone's talking!'

I dropped the phone and stood, waiting for my brain to tell my body what to do.

Memaw yelled, 'Nick! I smell smoke! What's going on in there?'

'Nothing!' I yelled as I stuck my hand into a sea of extinguisher foam to retrieve my phone.

Molly said, 'They called him . . .'

I pulled out my phone and yelled, 'What?'

'They called him Your Awesomeness!' said Molly.

I checked the cam again. It showed Karl reflected in the window outside the classroom.

I said, "Your Awesomeness? That sounds like he's some sort of . . .'

I don't think I'd ever seen a smile that wide.

'Oh my,' said Memaw from the kitchen door.

'It's me!' yelled Mum from the front door. 'I forgot my phone. Where is everybody?'

Memaw shook her head. 'You are so doomed.'

CHAPTER 12

I was grounded to my room. Not exactly the worst thing in the world.

MOLLY! LOOK OUT! THERE'S A SQUIDBOT RIGHT BEHIND YOU!

We were taking a video game break from the MLEZ-Karl situation. Which, with Molly, isn't really much of a break.

'No! No! No!' I yelled into my mic. 'The only way to get into Squidbot Headquarters is through the plumbing vent!'

'Wait,' said Molly into my earpiece. 'Why do Squidbots need plumbing?'

Game over. Again.

'I don't understand the point of this game,' said Molly.

'To have FUN!' I screamed.

'Nick, what are you doing?' asked Mum from behind me.

I wheeled around as I tried to casually slip off my headset.

I shrugged. 'Nothing.'

Mum hit me with her brain-penetrating laser stare. 'Uh-uh. Kids who almost burn the house down lose the right to shrug and say, "Nothing." And the right to play video games.'

Busted.

'What's going on with you? A mac 'n' cheese fire? A note from Dr Daniels that says you're refusing to show your work?'

'I just . . . there's a lot . . . It's fine. I can handle it.'

'Like you handled Memaw?'

'I got distracted by . . . ' I noticed a suitcase backpack by the door. It looked really familiar. 'Are you going somewhere?'

'No. That's your new roller backpack. No more bruised shoulders.'

I knew I'd seen it before. 'No!' I cried. 'That's just like Karl's. I can't be seen with—'

'Hey, I'll let you in on a little secret, buster. . . .

'Now we're going to have to hire someone we can't afford to look after Memaw.'

'Don't worry about me!' yelled Memaw from downstairs. 'I'll just eat pizza crumbs out of the recliner.'

Mum rubbed her forehead. 'I have no idea who we can get to help her at such short notice.'

Help her? Helper! WAIT! That's it!

'A helper monkey!' I cried.

Mum put her hand on my forehead. 'Do you have a fever?'

'No. Karl's mum works for this place that

trains monkeys to help people who can't do stuff. And it's free!' I reached for my phone. 'It's called the Monkey See and Do Centre. Here, I'll show you the website.'

Mum pulled her hand back. 'There's no way—'

'I like monkeys!' yelled Memaw from downstairs.

Mum yelled back, 'You don't have a vote on this!'

'Hey, I'm the one with the broken butt!' yelled Memaw. 'And I like my chances of survival better with the monkey.'

OUCH!

GRRR!

I pointed at my phone. 'It can't hurt to look, right?'

Mum looked at me, then at the door, then back at me. 'You said it's free?'

Memaw yelled, 'Free is your mum's favourite four-letter word. She'd go for a helper zombie if it were free and mopped floors and cleaned toilets.'

'Quiet, Mother! No monkey, and that's final!' shouted Mum.

'We'll see!' yelled Memaw.

It was a text from Molly.

Molly: You still there? Check on Karl again?

'Give me that,' said Mum. 'Maybe two weeks
without it will clear up your confusion about
what's important around here.'
'But . . .'
Mum's eyes narrowed. I handed her the phone.
'Is there something wrong with Karl?' asked
Mum.
Other than some freaky masked kid calling
him Your Awesomeness and making him some
sort of king?

SPORKS →

DOES THIS
MAKE MY
HEAD LOOK
BIGGER
THAN MY
BUTT?

'No,' I said to Mum. 'Karl's fine.'

CHAPTER 13

The next morning before school, Molly and I stood in front of my locker.

Molly pointed at my new roller backpack. 'That looks just like—'

'I don't want to talk about it,' I said. 'What are we going to do about Karl?'

'What can we do?' asked Molly. 'If he Karl-ifies everything, everyone in the school will hate him.'

'We have to save him from himself.'

'Save who?' said Becky and Simone as they walked up.

Simone spotted my freakish backpack. 'I like it. It's fashion backwards. Just like Karl's.'

I gritted my teeth.

'Is it Karl we're saving?' said Becky. 'He stopped me in the hall and asked me what I thought about the cafeteria changing to an all vegan menu.'

Molly and I looked at each other. We nodded. Then we told them everything.

'The school will revolt!' cried Simone.

THIS COULD BE
BAD. MUCH
WORSE THAN
WHEN YOU
DESTROYED THE
CAFETORIUM.

OR WHEN YOU
BULLIED YOURSELF.

OR WHEN YOU
YOU RUINED THE
FIELD TRIP TO
EGYPTOPOLIS.

ENOUGH!

'I get it,' I said. 'I agree. We have to rescue
Karl from MLEZ.'

'But how?' asked Molly.

'Just talk him out of it,' said Becky.

I shook my head. '"Oh, hey, Karl. You know,
you're really not cut out to lead a super-secret
group that sort of controls the school. We think
you'd be happier getting hung by your pants from
a coat hook."'

'Well, not like that,' said Becky.

'We could rat out MLEZ,' said Simone.

I said, 'With what evidence? A kid we don't
know in an Emily Dickinson mask who might
be part of a secret group that controls the school
wants to put Karl in charge? Of EVERYTHING?'

'We'll think of something,' said Molly. 'Class is about to start. We've gotta go.'

I was about to follow when I heard the voice of my ex-bully and locker-stuffer-in-er behind me.

'Dude! Help me out!'

'Roy?'

I turned around. Roy was walking up to me. Down the hall stood his Future Inmates of America posse.

Roy said. 'You see Dougie back there? The stupid one?'

That didn't really narrow it down.

'He's challenging me to a prank-off, and I need your help.'

'A prank-off?' I asked.

'Whoever pulls the biggest, baddest stunt gets to be leader.'

'What do you want me to do about it?'

Roy pointed at my locker.

'Seriously?'

'I'll owe ya.'

'Big time!'

'Whatever. Just make it look good.'

I rolled my eyes as I put my hands up. 'Dude! Please! Don't shove me into my locker!'

'Shut up, loser! You're going in!' yelled Roy.

I fake-struggled while Roy fake-shoved me into my locker and slammed the door.

I listened to Roy say, 'What do you have to say now, Dougie? You think you can top this? Just try and find your own tiny kid to stuff into a locker. This one's mine!'

Gee thanks, Roy.

As I waited to get out, I felt something digging into my back. I reached behind and . . .

DORIS!!

What's Doris doing in my locker? I didn't put her here. That means someone else did. Someone who wanted me to find it. Or someone who wanted Mr Dupree to see me find it – and think I took it!

'Someone is trying to set me up!' I said out loud.

But who? Wait. MLEZ? Sure, they've done strange stuff like this before, but it's always been to help me. Doris in my locker does not help me!

'Nick! Are you in there again?' said Mr Dupree from the hall.

Did you know when you scream really loud in your head it still seriously hurts? A lot.

I had about three seconds before Mr Dupree opened my locker.

'Just a second! I'm not decent!' I said as I furiously stuffed Doris into my backpack.

Mr Dupree said, 'You're not *what*?'

I barely got Doris stowed before Mr Dupree opened the locker.

He stared at me. 'Not decent?'

I stared at my shoes. 'I farted.'

Mr Dupree groaned, then waved his hand in the air. 'Come on. You know the drill.'

He helped me out and we started walking

down the hall to Dr Daniels's office. Mr Dupree
shook his head and said, 'You haven't seen Doris,
have you?'

'No,' I lied.

'Keep looking. Sooner or later whoever took her
will slip up.'

When I got to the office, I had to wait for Dr Daniels. I reached in my pocket to text Molly that I'd found Doris when . . .

Dr Daniels walked up. 'Nick! Exactly who I wanted to see.'

I said, 'You *want* to see me?'

'I . . . ah . . . umm . . . '

I guess my question confused her.

I don't know if Dr Daniels was ever a cat groomer, but I bet she'd be good at it.

It took her a few seconds to figure out an answer. 'Well, I can't help you if I don't see you. Now can I?'

Great. She's not giving up on me. Sorry, cats.

'Anyway,' she said. 'I have amazing news! You *can't* show your work!'

'I know,' I said.

'No, I mean, your brain doesn't work like everyone else's.'

Memaw's been saying that forever.

'You're a visual-spatial learner! Isn't that great!'

'Huh?'

'I was talking about you with some colleagues. One suggested I look into VS learning.'

'Talking about me?'

'I've set you up with a learning specialist to help you before school. She'll get you showing your work in no time! Aren't you excited? '

Not really.

CHAPTER 15

I had a lot of things on my mind when I got home after school. How were we going to save Karl from himself? Was it really MLEZ that planted Doris in my locker? Was MLEZ trying to set me up because we were getting close to figuring out who it was? Does MLEZ hate me now? How do I give Doris back to Mr Dupree without him thinking I took her in the first place?

The one thing I didn't have on my mind was . . .

. . . getting freaked out by a screaming monkey.

I said, 'But Mum said no monkey!'

'Sometimes your mother needs a little push to know what she wants.'

'You mean, what *you* want?'

'Bob's a spider monkey,' said Memaw. 'He's from the rain forests in South America. Isn't he cute?'

Annoying is a better word.

'ARE YOU KIDDING ME?!' said Mum from behind me.

'No! He is not!' answered Mum.

'He does dishes,' cooed Memaw.

'He hoovers,' said Memaw.

Mum said, 'I WILL NOT HAVE A MONKEY IN THIS— Wait. What's he doing?'

Bob was doing the one thing my mother couldn't handle.

'He's crying,' said Mum. 'Stop crying! Make him stop crying!'

Memaw opened a booklet in her lap. 'I don't know that command. Wait. Here it is. It's . . . *Stay.*'

Mum threw her arms up. 'Fine. Keep him. But if I find even one monkey hair in my meat loaf, he's gone!'

Even though Bob was seriously creepy, he was going to help Memaw and free me up to deal with my own problems.

Maybe things were looking up – at least at home. It gave me hope that things might go better at school tomorrow.

CHAPTER 16

Despite what my annoying imaginary superhero said, I kept hope alive – all through the evening, into the next morning, and right up until before school when I met Ms Kapezki, my volunteer visual-spatial-learning specialist.

Ms Kapezki stared at me. 'Why aren't you excited?'

'Um, I'm excited,' I lied.

Then she flashed a smile so blinding, it could have been seen from space.

Ms Kapezki dropped her enormous handbag onto the desk. She reached her whole arm in and pulled out a stack of flash cards that looked like a unicorn had thrown up on them.

She flashed another blinding smile. 'Let's get started.'

She dove back into the bag and came out with one of those crazy scary-eyed dolls drowning in ribbons and bows. 'Now, sweet pea, I hear you're quite the little maths tutor, so I want you to show Brynleigh Anne here how you did the problem.'

'Huh?' I said.

'Tell her, you silly goose!'

'Two times seven equals fourteen,' I said.

'No, sugar plum. The answer in your silly old strange head!'

'I see the times tables.'

Ms Kapezki cheered. 'That's SO awesome! Isn't that awesome? I think it's awesome. Please tell me you think it's awesome.'

I nodded. 'It's awesome.'

'YEAH! Now, lollipop, how are we going to get that picture in your head on the paper?'

I had no idea. I just hoped it didn't involve her saying awesome again.

'What if we do something super silly and solve the problem backwards?'

'O-kay?'

'Write down what's the reverse of two times seven equals fourteen.'

I wrote down:

$$14/2$$

'Perfect! So how do we get $2x=14$ to look like $x=14/2$?

I said, 'You divide both sides by two.'

$$2X/2 = 14/2$$
$$X = 7$$

'And x equals?'

'I already told you. Seven!'

She pointed at the paper. 'Sweetie, you just showed your work.'

I showed my work? Wait. What?

I stared at the paper. Yes, there was actual work on the paper. But the truth was, I didn't so much show my work as I *slowed* my work.

'See? Easy Kapezki! Next time we'll try a harder problem.'

When we were finished, she gathered all her stuff and walked to the door. 'Bye, sweetie!' She flashed yet another blinding smile. Great. I'd be seeing spots for the rest of the day.

'Nick!'

I squinted. Becky was at the door. Behind the spots.

'We were going to talk to Karl,' said Becky. 'But he ran into the second-floor boys' toilets. You have to get him out before school starts.'

I said, 'Why can't you get him out?'

'We're not going in there!'

'It's just Karl!'

'It's gross!'

'It's the same as your toilets.'

'No. It's not.'

Okay. Maybe not.

CHAPTER 17

Molly and Simone were waiting outside the toilets.

'We don't have a lot of time before the bell rings,' said Molly. 'You need to hurry and get Karl out of the toilets now!'

The words *hurry, Karl,* and *toilets,* do not belong in the same sentence.

I said, 'What's the rush?'

BEFORE HE WENT IN, HE TRIED TO GET US TO TASTE ONE OF THESE.

TOFU TOT ←

That was enough convincing for me. I pushed myself into the toilets.'Karl?'

'Present,' said Karl from inside one of the

cubicles.

I said, 'Hey, the girls and I need to talk to you before school starts.'

Karl said, 'Sure. Just give me a second.'

I said, 'No, we need to talk right now.'

'I know you've been following me.'

'What?'

'I've never had anyone follow me around before. It's sort of like I'm leading a really short parade except nobody's watching and there're no fat guys in silly hats driving tiny cars.'

'Um . . . '

'And I know you and everyone in Safety Patrol know about "Your Awesomeness".'

'You do?'

'At first I was excited about it. Nobody has ever asked me to be in charge of anything. I mean, this is my chance to really help kids in this school. It feels good. Like in *NanoNerd #51* when the Dwarf-Sloths of Ruptkis 12 made NanoNerd their ruler.

'Then I thought maybe

it wasn't such a good idea because everyone might think I'd be a bad leader 'cause I could make everyone eat Tofu Tots. But then I wondered, 'Who doesn't like Tofu Tots?"

I started to raise my hand.

'We're waiting!' yelled Molly from outside the bathroom door.

I went over to the sinks and turned on a tap to speed things up.

'I made some at home. They're in my backpack. Try one,' said Karl.

Not in this lifetime.

Karl continued, 'Anyway, I thought if I'm in charge of MLEZ, maybe I could change things.'

'What things?' I said.

'But before I do any of that,' said Karl, 'there's something very important I need to do first.'

What? Tattoo 'Mock Me' on your forehead?

'You know Humpty Dumpty didn't fall, right?'

Huh?

'He was pushed. The nursery rhyme covered it up. It was no accident. Someone didn't want Humpty on that wall.'

Okay. Where's he going with this?

'I feel like Humpty up on that wall. I want to be up there. It's my chance to show everyone I'm not afraid of heights anymore. But there's always someone who wants to knock me off. They want me down on the ground with all the king's horses and all the king's men.'

I was officially lost.

'I need help up on the wall. I need someone to watch my back. Someone like you or Molly.'

I said, 'Watch your back?'

'I want you and Molly to join me in MLEZ.'

Wait. What?

He wasn't supposed to say that! He was supposed to make it easy for us to help him by talking him *out* of running the school. But now he wants us to help him by *actually* helping him run the school?

He's so INCONSIDERATE!

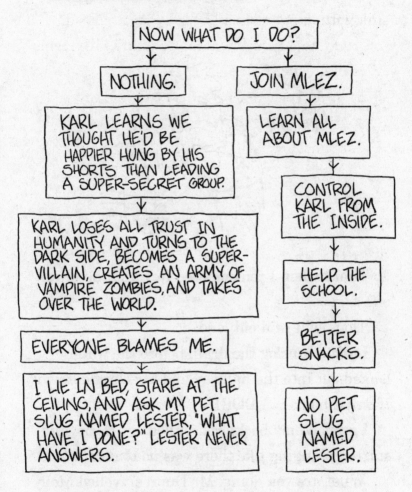

NOW WHAT DO I DO?

NOTHING.

KARL LEARNS WE THOUGHT HE'D BE HAPPIER HUNG BY HIS SHORTS THAN LEADING A SUPER-SECRET GROUP.

KARL LOSES ALL TRUST IN HUMANITY AND TURNS TO THE DARK SIDE, BECOMES A SUPER-VILLAIN, CREATES AN ARMY OF VAMPIRE ZOMBIES, AND TAKES OVER THE WORLD.

EVERYONE BLAMES ME.

I LIE IN BED, STARE AT THE CEILING, AND ASK MY PET SLUG NAMED LESTER, "WHAT HAVE I DONE?" LESTER NEVER ANSWERS.

JOIN MLEZ.

LEARN ALL ABOUT MLEZ.

CONTROL KARL FROM THE INSIDE.

HELP THE SCHOOL.

BETTER SNACKS.

NO PET SLUG NAMED LESTER.

Before I could figure out what to do, Karl said, 'Why is there water coming into the cubicles?'

I looked down. I was standing in a puddle. I

turned to the sinks. One of them was overflowing!

I tried to turn off the tap, but it wouldn't turn off. Someone had messed with it and clogged the sink with . . .

That's when I remembered Roy and the prank-off.

'Dougie!' I said out loud.

I had to unclog the drain before the water leaked out into the hallway and Mr Dupree saw it. If only I had a . . . DORIS!

I grabbed my backpack, pulled out Doris, and started plunging like there was no tomorrow.

'What are you doing, Mr Dupree?' yelled Molly from out in the hall.

'No!' I said.

'My job,' said Mr Dupree. 'There's a leak

coming from the toilets.'

I turned around. The water was already out the door.

I had two seconds to get rid of the plunger before Mr Dupree came in. I looked left, right, down, and finally . . .

That's when everything went into super slow motion.

It stuck! It really stuck. For once, a plan of mine worked! I couldn't wait to tell everybody. But when the bathroom door opened, I realised I couldn't tell anybody.

CHAPTER 18

'Boys,' said Molly as she surveyed the mess.

Becky and Simone nodded together. 'Mm-hm.'

'It wasn't me,' I said. 'The sink was already clogged. I just turned on the water. But then I couldn't turn it off.'

Mr Dupree fished a sock out of the sink drain. Inside was a label. 'Dougie,' read Mr Dupree.

I nodded. 'The stupid one.'

It was the bell for first class.

We all started to leave when Mr Dupree said, 'Nick, Molly, what's happening with the search for Doris?'

Molly and I stopped as the others left.

'We haven't seen her,' I said. 'We've asked around, but no one's seen her.'

Mr Dupree turned to Molly. 'You checked everywhere?'

Molly said, 'She must be around here somewhere!'

That's when I looked up and saw . . .

But where? Wait. Stuff like that only happens with . . .

MLEZ?

Mr Dupree stared at me. 'You look like you've seen a ghost.'

I don't know. Maybe MLEZ is a ghost. But I wasn't going to say that to Mr Dupree. I had only one move. It's like Memaw likes to say . . .

I shrugged.

Mr Dupree shook his head and headed for the door. He said, 'Please. Find Doris!'

We slowly turned around and stared at, well, a ghost.

Sort of.

Molly said, 'Wait. You're um . . . '

'Alice Frektner,' she said.

'Who?' I said.

Molly said, 'Wait. I know you. You're the invisible girl I tried to get the OMGs to help out!'

'I appreciated the effort,' said Alice.

I said, '*You're* part of MLEZ?'

Molly pulled her yearbook out of her backpack. 'But we eliminated everybody. We went through every page.'

Alice smiled. 'Look again. Look *closely* this time.'

We did look again. We searched and searched and searched. Nothing. Then . . .

Molly said, 'We missed you!'

'That happens a lot,' said Alice.

Who better to be part of a super-secret group than a girl who's INVISIBLE!

I said, 'No wonder we could never figure out who MLEZ was.'

'You said "us". There are others?' said Molly.

'Of course. And we're all really happy you passed the test,' she said.

'What test?' I said.

Alice smiled. 'You didn't talk Karl out of being part of MLEZ.'

Molly and I shared a look. 'Yeah. Right. Of course . . . not,' we mumbled.

'We couldn't be sure,' said Alice. 'You two haven't always been nice to Karl.'

Wait. That's not true. We like Karl. You know, except when he's being really weird. Which, now that I think about it, is most of the time. Which, I guess means . . .

'Wait a second,' said Molly. 'What about Doris showing up in Nick's locker? Was that you? Did you steal her?'

'I borrowed her,' said Alice as she handed Doris back to me. 'Just some insurance, in case you tried to interfere with Karl.'

'You were prepared to set me up to protect Karl?' I asked.

Alice smiled again. 'Karl is smart. Karl is brave. Karl is sweet and kind. He's the only kid at this school who is completely comfortable with being himself. What else could you want in a leader?'

I thought. 'How about not force-feeding me Tofu Tots?'

Alice said, 'Karl wanted the two of you in MLEZ from the start. He trusts you. And now the rest of us can too.'

CHAPTER 19

I got home from school and went straight to my room. I was still grounded. No video games. No phone. It was like when Memaw was a little girl. . . .

ALL WE HAD TO PLAY WITH WERE FINGER-NAIL CLIPPINGS AND A PIECE OF YARN.

I was about to die of boredom when my computer beeped. It was a video-chat invite from Molly.

I clicked connect, and Molly appeared on my screen.

'We need to talk about Alice,' she said. 'That girl is seriously scary.'

'Yeah, but she's just watching out for Karl. You know, just like us.'

'No. We weren't setting anybody up for stealing Doris.'

'I guess she *really* likes Karl.'

'And we were totally going to talk Karl out of MLEZ.'

'I know. We didn't pass her test.'

She's such a stealth mum! She never wears the Mum Early Detection System I gave her for her birthday.

'It's no big deal,' I answered.

'Hm. Dr Daniels called me about your before-school sessions with Ms Kapezki.'

Whatever happened to guidance counsellor–student confidentiality? Kids have no privacy! Or rights!

OR CREDIT CARDS.

AND WE CAN'T DRIVE A CAR.

It's not fair!

Mum said, 'Dr Daniels explained about the BASS test and how she's working with promising students to help them reach their full potential. She told me how you need to show your work so you'll help the school get a higher rating.'

'I never showed my work and I turned out fine!' yelled Memaw from downstairs.

Mum said, 'The jury's still out on that, Mother!' She turned to me. 'On top of the BASS test, you've also got your Schoolseum project.'

'Everything is fine!' I said. 'Memaw is helping me with my project.'

Mostly by keeping our dog, Janice, from eating it.

RIDE 'EM, BOB!

TAJ MAHAL OUT OF SUGAR CUBES.

'And Ms Kapezki is actually getting me to show my work,' I added.

I told Mum about this super-hard problem Mr Wickler gave me.

Amy is twice as old as Jenny. Five years ago, Amy was three times as old as Jenny. Find Jenny's age. Show your work!

At first I just stared at the problem like I normally do and waited for the answer. But then the picture in my head started showing up on the board.

For the first time, I showed my work in front of Mr Wickler!

I figured he'd do some sort of alien worms-for-brains victory dance, but he just stood there for a long time until he finally said . . .

I said, 'Are you okay, Mr Wickler?'

That was when he did something I'd never seen an adult do.

He shrugged.

I didn't tell Mum about the shrugging. I didn't need her going to school and complaining about teachers not showing enthusiasm.

Instead I flashed her my best trust-me smile and said, 'Seriously. Everything's under control.'

Mum hugged me and said, 'Why is it when you say, "Everything's under control" all I hear is "My socks are on fire?"'

CHAPTER 20

I said, 'Where is everybody?'

'This *is* everybody,' said Alice.

I looked around. It was just me, Molly, Karl, Alice, and a couple of chess sets in Outdoor Temporary Classroom #7 for our first MLEZ meeting.

'This is everybody in *your* group,' said Alice. 'There are lots of other MLEZ groups. Each is separate from the other. This way if one group is discovered, it can't rat out the others.'

'Has it always been like that?' asked Molly.

Alice nodded. She explained that MLEZ was started a million years ago by this girl named Ethel. Ethel got tired of never getting picked for dodgeball because she was invisible – like Alice. Ethel recruited other outcast kids who were also plain or bullied or who didn't fit in, and eventually they pretty much ran the school.

'So this is the Chess Club?'

We all turned around to see Mr Dupree standing at the door.

We nodded and smiled like, 'Sure we're in Chess Club! Why wouldn't be in Chess Club? Chess Club is awesome!'

Mr Dupree said, 'Wow. And so many members! Did I ever tell you about the time I played chess against a robot?'

Groan.

'It was years ago,' Mr Dupree began. 'The Chessbot 5000 was primitive by today's standards.'

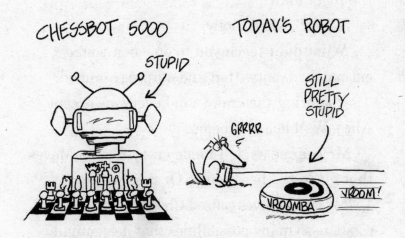

CHESSBOT 5000   TODAY'S ROBOT

STUPID

STILL
PRETTY
STUPID

GRRRR

VROOMBA   VROOM!

'Did he shoot lasers with his eyes?' asked Karl.

'No. He just played chess, Karl,' said Mr

Dupree.

'What about Twister?' asked Karl.

'No Twister. Now let me tell the story.'

Mr Dupree continued, 'The Chessbot 5000 was programmed to look at thousands of possible moves and pick the best one.

'I got off to a rocky start. I lost my queen in the first ten moves.'

Karl sighed. 'Poor queen.'

Mr Dupree continued, 'But I knew something the robot didn't.'

'What?' asked Molly.

'What did I teach you to do when you're outmatched, outwitted and outprogrammed?'

'You bring the crazy,' said everyone except Alice. We'd heard it before.

Mr Dupree said, 'I made crazy moves. Moves that made no chess sense. Or robot sense.

'My crazy moves caused Chessbot 5000 to compute so many possibilities that it eventually . . . '

Karl sighed. 'Poor robot.'

'The robot lost the match because it couldn't

predict a move no one had ever made before. You can't predict crazy.'

'Huh?' I said.

'He means, when we play chess, we should expect what we don't expect,' said Alice.

Mr Dupree said, 'Or whenever you're playing to win. Now, have you seen Doris?'

We all shook our heads.

Mr Dupree said, 'Keep looking. I can't give the keynote address on plunger safety at the Annual State Janitors Convention in three weeks without her.'

There was so much epic random weirdness in that previous sentence that none of us said a word.

After Mr Dupree left, Alice shook her head. 'I think Mr Dupree—'

It was Karl's phone. 'No!' he moaned. 'Stanley's flown away again.'

'Rocket Park?' asked Molly.

Karl said, 'I made him a bubble wrap vest, but he won't wear it. He thinks it makes him look fat.'

After Karl left, I looked at Alice. 'What were you saying about Mr Dupree?'

'I think he's on to us,' said Alice. 'I think he's saying we can hide all we want, but we can't hide from him.'

'I'm not sure he's saying that,' said Molly.

'Me neither. And why are we hiding at all?' I asked.

Alice stared at me. 'We can't do what we do in the open. MLEZ has to stay a secret.'

'Secrets are hard to keep,' said Molly.

'Secrets have kept this school safe for a long time,' said Alice. 'I'm not going to let some busybody hippie janitor get in the way of everything we've built. It's too important. We have to do something to get Mr Dupree off our backs.'

Molly turned to me. 'You could start by giving Doris back to him.'

I said, 'I'm going to. I haven't had a chance. I mean, I can't just give her to him.'

'Exactly,' said Alice.

'No, he'll think I took her,' I said. 'I'll just leave

her somewhere he can find her.'

Alice shook her head. 'No, we leave her where he's sure he's already looked, so he'll think she was there the whole time and he just forgot.'

'Or he'll think someone's messing with him,' said Molly.

'Not if other things go missing and then show up later in places where he knows he's already looked,' said Alice. 'He'll be so busy trying to figure out which end is up that he won't pay any attention to us.'

'That's mean!' cried Molly.

NO. THAT'S YOUR FIRST MLEZ ASSIGNMENT.

CHAPTER 21

'We're not going to do it, right?'

'Of course we're not going to do it,' I told Molly as we walked down the empty school hallway. 'We're just going to put the plunger where he can find it and take off.'

'Alice really is a little cray-cray,' said Molly.

'A little?'

'What are we going to tell her?'

'That we messed with Mr Dupree's head and he's all confused and he won't bother MLEZ anymore.'

'What if she doesn't believe us?'

'Why wouldn't she believe us? She trusts us now.'

'But we lied about talking Karl out of joining MLEZ.'

I shook my head. 'But she doesn't know that.'

'What about after this?' said Molly. 'Are we staying in MLEZ?'

'I don't know,' I said.

And I didn't. I'd been mad when Alice didn't pick me to join MLEZ. But messing with Mr Dupree was going too far. Maybe we could reason with Alice in the future. Maybe not.

We arrived at the door that led down to Safety Patrol Headquarters (and Mr D's janitorial supplies).

'Is the coast clear?' I asked.

Molly looked down the hall. 'All clear.'

'Hand me the plunger.'

Molly opened my new lame-o rolling backpack. 'Um . . . why do you have a dozen cans of tuna? And a doll's head? And a toy piano?'

'What?'

IT'S KARL'S BACKPACK!

THAT'S A LOT OF EXTRA UNDERWEAR.

Karl must have taken my backpack when he left. 'That means . . .

KARL HAS DORIS!

CHAPTER 22

Molly and I met the rest of Safety Patrol at Karl's house after school.

'Why are we here again?' asked Becky,

WERE GOING TO GET MR. DUPREE'S PLUNGER.

KARL'S HOUSE →

'Then we're going to put it where Mr D can find it,' I continued. 'Later we'll figure out what to do about Alice.'

'Alice?' asked Becky.

Molly and I filled Becky and Simone in on Alice.

'Wait,' said Simone. 'Why are you two in MLEZ and we're not?'

Becky nodded. 'Yeah.'

'How do we know you're *not* part of MLEZ and in a separate group?' I said.

Becky rolled her eyes. 'We're not.'

I said, 'That's what you're supposed to say.'

Molly glared at me. 'Stop it.' She turned to Becky and Simone. 'I know how you feel. I felt the same way when MLEZ picked Karl and not me. But then Karl picked me and now Alice is scaring me and I feel stupid for feeling left out.'

'You saved us from feeling stupid,' said Simone.

Simone looked up at Karl's house. 'I don't know. We could get caught inside.'

'Why can't we just swap your backpacks tomorrow?' asked Becky.

'Karl will find Doris by then and give her to Mr Dupree,' I said.

'Isn't that what you're going to do anyway?' asked Simone.

'I'm going to leave Doris where Mr Dupree can find her. If Karl just hands her to him, there'll be questions like, "Where did you find her and how long have you had her and why do you look so guilty?"'

Karl doesn't do so well under pressure.

The thing about working with girls is there's entirely too much talking and not enough doing!

'ENOUGH!' I yelled. 'We are going into Karl's room and we are going to get that plunger!'

'Dude, chill!' said Molly.

Becky glared at me. 'If you're going to yell, I'm going home.'

'We're *all* going home,' snapped Simone.

The other thing about working with girls is they're impossible to boss around unless you ask nicely.

'Okay, good,' I said. 'Becky, you stay down here and keep a lookout. If you see anything, hoot like an owl.'

'I can moo like a cow better,' said Becky.

'Do you see any cows around here?' I said.

'I don't see any owls, either,' said Becky.

I threw up my arms. 'Fine. Whatever. MOO!'

When the plunger-sticking-to-the-ceiling thing actually worked, I figured my luck with plans had changed. Nope.

I don't understand. They always work so well in my head.

Not so much anywhere else.

All we had to do was sneak in Karl's room and swap the backpacks while Becky distracted Karl downstairs. Simple, right?

It's never simple.

The first problem: Karl was taking a nap. I know! Who takes naps? What is he, four?

With Karl sleeping, I had to call Becky off at the front door.

Nick: KARL'S TAKING A NAP! DON'T RING THE DOORBELL!

Becky: You don't have to yell.

The second problem: Karl's room isn't like a normal twelve-year-old's room. Karl's room has an alarm.

'Is that you?' said Karl. 'You must have got my letter. Is the fleece cape in royal purple too much trouble? You can substitute with normal purple. No problem. I don't want to be a bother.'

Simone giggled.

Stanley sang, 'Batmobile lost a wheel. Joker ran away! Hey!'

'Now, Stanley, don't be rude,' said Karl. 'Santa, come out. I want to show you my sea monkeys. I taught them how to cha-cha!'

The sea monkeys! Of course!

Simone snorted again. Molly elbowed me in the ribs.

'You CAN talk!' said Karl. 'I knew it. How else can you count cha-cha steps? Can you *all* talk?' asked Karl.

I looked at Molly. Molly looked at Simone.

'Yes!' squeaked Molly.

'You bet!' chirped Simone.

Karl started clapping.

'I want you do something, Karl,' I said. 'I want you to um . . . sing . . . um . . . '

My mind went blank. I couldn't think of a
song!

'"Frère Jacques"? As a round?' said Karl.

Thank you, thank you, thank you, Karl, for
being so weird!

'Yes!' I said. 'Sing "Frère Jacques" as a round
with us!'

Karl cheered. 'This is the happiest day of my
life!'

Okay, that's too weird.

'You go first,' said Karl. 'No. Wait. I'll go first.
Unless you want to go first. Do you want to go
first?'

I squeaked, 'You go first, Karl.'

Karl began singing. 'Frère Jacques, frère
Jacques.'

We sang together until Karl fell back to sleep.
It only took an hour.

CHAPTER 24

The next morning I came downstairs to see Memaw and Bob watching Memaw's second favourite show on the Black-and-White channel.

It's about this freaky dog that's always saving this kid named Brandon who's always getting stuck in mines and clothes dryers.

In every episode Jack runs to get help from someone who happens to speak fluent dog.

And in every episode, Brandon is saved before the mine collapses or someone plugs in the dryer.

'Brandon is saved! Now I can start my day!'
Memaw cheered.

I said, 'I'm happy for you.'

Memaw eyed me. 'What is it now?'

'Nothing.'

Memaw shot me her you-will-tell-me-everything-or-I-will-force-you-to-go-underwear-shopping-even-though-I-said-I-never-would look.

I confessed. 'The BASS test is today!'

'Stupid testing,' said Memaw as she shook her head. 'They say Albert Einstein said, "Everyone's a genius. But if you judge a fish on its ability to climb a tree, it will live its whole life believing that it is stupid."'

I had no idea what she was talking about, but I'd heard of Einstein. We learned about him in science class.

ALBERT EINSTEIN

FIGURED OUT LIGHT IS BENT BY GRAVITY.

GRRRRRRR...

PERMANENT BED HEAD

AS STUFF SPEEDS UP, TIME SLOWS DOWN RELATIVE TO AN OBSERVER.

ZIP!

STUFF GETS REALLY FAT WHEN IT GOES AS FAST AS LIGHT.

ZIP!

1879 – 1955
THEORETICAL PHYSICIST.
DEVELOPED GENERAL
THEORY OF RELATIVITY.

SAID, 'GOD DOESN'T PLAY DICE WITH THE UNIVERSE.'

YAHTZEE!

?

I said, 'It's not that big a deal. If I show my work, I'll do fine.'

'You know Einstein never showed his work,' said Memaw.

'Huh?

'E equals MC squared?'

VERY GOOD, ALBERT. BUT NEXT TIME SHOW YOUR WORK.

$E = Mc^2$

LATER

WELCOME TO COSTLO.

135

I said, 'I don't think they'll let me skip the test because Mr Einstein didn't show his work.'

Memaw sighed. 'I know, sweetie. It isn't fair. When life gives you beetroots, you make beetroot juice. Then you choke it down and try not to barf.'

What?

'Come here and give Bob and me a big squeeze.'

CHAPTER 25

I stared deep into Ms Kapezki's eyes as I stood outside the classroom.

'Are you ready for the BASS test, sunshine?' she asked.

I nodded. She hugged me and I lost all sense of time and space.

When she released me to the light, she said, 'Remember, sugar, the work you are showing is the work your silly-willy brain is seeing.'

I nodded.

'Now, go kick this test's butt! Remember, EASY KAPEZKI!'

I smiled and walked into the classroom. I was confident. I had this. Absolutely NOTHING could stop me.

Mr Wickler is my examiner? Seriously? Not fair!

'Good luck today,' he said.

Yeah, right. Like he wants me to do well. I took a deep breath. I told myself to relax. I still had this. And I did. Right up until . . .

I was doomed. Again.

'Missing something?'

I looked up. Mr Wickler was smiling down at me. I knew what those body-snatching alien worms in his head were telling him to say. . . .

Mr Wickler wanted me to fail. It explained why he looked so disappointed when I finally showed my work. He was pure evil. He was—

'Here,' said Mr Wickler as he handed me a pencil. 'Lucky I had a spare. Good luck.'

Wait. It must be some sort of trick. The pencil looked okay. It wasn't one of those cheap ones made from compressed leaves. Could it be? Was Mr Wickler human after all?

I flipped open my test booklet. First there was a story about colossal squids that are bigger than giant squids but smaller than Arkansas.

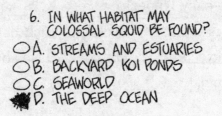

Easy Kapezki.

The next section was writing. I had to write two pages about a time when I was right. Which was hard, because there were too many good examples to pick just one.

I wrote about the time Memaw and I were at the supermarket betting on what shoppers would buy.

There was this dressed-up guy in the crisp aisle. Memaw bet on Organic Sea Salt Crisps. I bet on Mr Saltysnack Supercheesy Bacon-n-Mayo Crisps.

Way-too-easy Kapezki!

Next was the maths section, which had a lot of multiple choice and . . . Oh no . . . Two show-your-work problems!

I took a deep breath, closed my eyes, and tried to clear my mind.

I read the first problem to myself. 'If Sam's lunch costs $2.25, then how much would he need for five days of lunches?'

I knew the answer was $11.25, but I also knew I wasn't finished. So I did what Ms Kapezki taught me: I *slowed* my work to *show* my work.

Super-mega easy Kapezki!

The second problem was harder. It was an intersecting Venn diagram showing a pizza topping survey of seventy-five people.

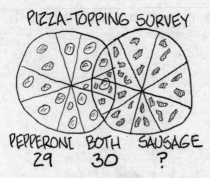

PIZZA-TOPPING SURVEY

PEPPERONI   BOTH   SAUSAGE
   29   30   ?

Again, I knew the answer was sixteen. And again I put the picture in my head on the answer sheet: 75 − 59 = 16. I wrote down the answer, but then everything went . . . wrong.

I scratched through the work. Then I wrote down: 75 − (29 + 30) = 16. It sort of looked right, but I wasn't sure.

'One minute left,' said Mr Wickler.

I looked up. 'NO!'

He said, 'Is there a problem, Nick?'

I didn't answer. I was too busy drawing pizzas as fast as I could. $29 + 30 + X = 75$, then $59 + X = 75$, add 59 to each side . . . No. Wait. I'm supposed to subtract—

TIME!

NOOOOO!

Not-so-easy Kapezki.

$\mathbf{I}$ got the right answer! I did! I just got confused about exactly how I got the right answer. They'll understand. They'll give me credit. I'll get a good score. It won't be my fault if Boy Toyz doesn't perform.

But before I could start thinking about running away to a freak show . . .

... I saw Mr Dupree's mop bucket all alone outside the boys' toilets. Maybe I couldn't pass the BASS test, but at least I could return Doris.

All I had to do was put her down and keep walking, and Mr Dupree would never know who'd returned her.

I pulled Doris out of my roller backpack, walked over to the mop bucket, put her down, and ...

'We thought we could trust you,' said Alice. 'We thought you were like us. But you're not. You're not doing what I said to do. You don't really care about MLEZ and keeping the school safe. You just care about yourself.'

'No. You're wrong,' I said. 'I—'

'It's a good thing we had Plan B!'

'Plan B?'

I started to inch forward to grab Doris when Mr Dupree burst out of the boys' toilets.

'I . . . um . . . I did . . . um fine.' I said. There was only one thing I could do.

A mini-tsunami of water rushed down the hall straight toward a sixth-grader.

As Mr Dupree sloshed down the hall to rescue the kid, I turned and grabbed Doris from Alice.

I needed to get out of there fast. I got up, turned to shove Doris back into my backpack, but . . .

And so was Alice.

I was about to run, when I saw Molly standing
at the opposite end of the hall.

I tried not to think about how my plans never seemed to work. I tried to stay positive. I tried to remember another thing Memaw liked to say.

EVEN A BLIND ZOMBIE FINDS SOME BRAINS ONCE IN A WHILE.

NOD-NOD

But it didn't really help.

CHAPTER 27

'This isn't Doris,' said Mr Dupree.

SHE DOESN'T HAVE THE
NICK THE BALD GERMAN
FOREIGN MINISTER
PUT IN HER WHEN HE
WAS SHAVING AND
FORGOT SHE WAS ON
HIS HEAD.

But it was the same plunger – the one from my backpack. The same backpack Karl took by mistake. It HAD to be Mr Dupree's plunger. Unless . . .

BACK IN THE RESTROOM

HERE'S YOUR
PLUNGER
BACK.

. . . Alice handed me a fake plunger! That must have been 'Plan B!' She had the real one all along.

But . . . then why take my backpack?

Mr Dupree inspected the new plunger. Then he looked at me with a I-am-*seriously*-disappointed-in-you,-young-man look.

Normally, this would be a must-shrug mument. But the *serious* look of disappointment on Mr Dupree's face took all shrug options off the table. He deserved the truth.

Not that he would believe it.

'WHAT'S GOING ON HERE?' said Dr Daniels.

She was standing with her hands on her hips in the I-mean-business-and-I'm-not-kidding stance she learned at online guidance counsellor school.

Mr Dupree held up Doris. 'I found my plunger.'

Dr Daniels looked confused. 'I didn't know it was missing.'

Mr Dupree said, 'It was. And it's very important to me. These kids all know how important it is to me. And *somehow* it ended up in Nick's backpack.'

Dr Daniels looked at me. 'As though you're not in enough trouble already.'

What was that supposed to mean?

Mr Dupree said, 'Now they're trying to blame this all on Alice Frektner.'

'Who?' said Dr. Daniels.

'Plain girl? Blends in?' said Mr Dupree.

Dr Daniels shook her head. Then: 'Oh . . . OH! Right. I remember Alice. She's the sweet, shy girl I suggested wear brighter colours.'

Mr Dupree said, 'They claim she's a member of Emily.'

'MLEZ,' I said.

'That ghost you kids made up to explain things that happen at school you don't understand?' said Dr Daniels.

'MLEZ is not a ghost,' said Molly.

Dr Daniels stared at Karl for a second

before turning back to Mr Dupree. 'Alice? A mastermind? The girl hardly casts a shadow!'

'Which makes her perfect for the job,' I said under my breath.

Mr Dupree added some extra-serious to his already I-am-*seriously*-disappointed-in-you,-young-man look.

Dr Daniels nodded. 'One crisis at a time.' She held up my BASS answer sheet. 'First, Nick has to explain *this* to a BASS test official.'

'What?' I said. 'I showed my work!'

'But not for the answer you gave,' said Dr

Daniels.

'But I put down the right answer!' I said.

'I know, but they're not giving you credit, and the scores were tight. We need that answer to get an exemplary school rating.'

'And the Boy Toyz,' added Molly.

I said, 'You're saying we're one point short?'

Dr Daniels nodded again. 'Yes. And tomorrow night before the Schoolseum, we're going to meet with the BASS testing official and plead your case.'

That's when everyone stared at me and I tried to do what Alice makes look so easy.

I tried to disappear.

It's a lot harder than it looks.

CHAPTER 28

I couldn't sleep. It was one A.M. After staring at the bumps on my ceiling that I swear spelled out 'loser', I decided to go downstairs to eat a bowl of NanoPops.

I didn't find any NanoPops, but I did find a sleeping monkey, his belly stuffed with my Schoolseum project.

The fridge door opened behind me. It was Memaw, sitting in her wheelchair, reaching for a leftover slice of mac 'n' cheese pizza.

She looked at me. 'What? I don't have a problem.'

'Right,' I said.

She looked past me to Bob. 'Oh my.'

'It's ruined!' I said.

Memaw took a bite of her pizza. 'I'm 'o 'orry, 'ick. 'Ob's 'ust 'cheivous, 'ough 'e does 'ook 'omfortable.'

'The Schoolseum is tomorrow!'

Memaw swallowed. 'We'll think of something. Remember, every time a tornado rips a roof off, a sun-room is born.'

Huh?

'What class was your project for?'

'World History.'

Memaw stared at what was left of my Taj Mahal. After a few seconds she nodded.

'The Cercopes,' she said.

'What?'

She pulled her smartphone out of her housecoat pocket and handed it me. 'Look it up. It's your project!'

I looked up Cercopes. They're these freaky-looking monkey mischief-makers from Greek mythology.

SERIOUSLY FREAKY- LOOKING

'Thanks. I think.'

'Problem solved, then. Now, what are you doing downstairs?'

'Couldn't sleep.'

'Nightmares?'

I shook my head.

'Were you in your underwear? Was there any flying? Did a giant rabbit named Dave want to wrestle?'

'I *didn't* have a nightmare!'

'I guess that's just me. Doesn't matter. I know exactly what's going on.'

'Huh?'

Memaw shook her head. 'You couldn't hide from trouble in your own shadow.'

Then she told me everything I already knew. . . .

Memaw added, 'Mr Dupree doesn't think you stole Doris, but he doesn't believe all this Emily-Alice stuff either.'

'But it's true!'

'Even so. It's not your job to fix everything. Your job is to be a good kid and rub my neck when I ask!'

Bob started snoring.

Memaw said, 'You ever see anyone else besides Alice in MLEZ?'

'No, but that's on purpose so we can't rat out the other members.'

'Or there aren't any other members. Why all the secrecy?'

'She says if everyone knew who we were, we couldn't do what we do.'

'Then why invite you to join?'

'I don't know. She thought we could help?'

Memaw smiled. 'I think she wanted to show you what she was doing. I think she wanted to show *everyone* what she was doing!'

Wait. Show?

'You need to put her in a situation where she can't help but brag. You need to get her to—'

'SHOW HER WORK!' I cried.

'Yeah. Show her work,' said Memaw as she grabbed a dish towel, rolled herself over to a snoring Bob, and stood up shakily.

'But how?' I asked.

Memaw laid the dish towel across Bob, waking him. 'This will make a fine toga.'

'I should probably be doing that myself.'

'Don't worry. I'll let you take all the credit.'

Credit? Wait. That's it!

WE'LL TAKE THE CREDIT!

TOGA

You run. You hide. But no matter what you do, you can't escape your past. You try to change. You try new underwear. You start saying things like 'please' and 'thank you' and 'I can't wait to send a thank-you note!'

But none of it works. Because the past isn't interested in who you are now. Or who you're trying to be. Or how it's really, really going to be different this time. No. The past only cares about who you *were*. And the past never EVER forgets.

'*You* have a plan?' asked Molly.

'What?' I said.

It was the next evening at school. Molly, Karl, Becky, Simone and I were standing in the hall waiting for the Schoolseum to start.

Molly said, 'Your plans don't work out very well.'

'Or at all,' added Simone.

I said, 'Hey. We swapped Karl's and my backpacks the other night, didn't we?'

Karl looked confused. 'Wait. What?'

Oops.

Karl gasped. 'YOU were the sea monkeys! No wonder, when I asked them to sing "Frère Jacques", they looked at me like I spat in their aquarium.'

'Nick?' said Dr Daniels from behind me.

I turned around.

Perfect Phil used to date my mum. She stopped seeing him after he tried to make me repeat seventh grade for fake bullying because of some stupid Zero Tolerance policy.

Perfect Phil wasn't going to care that I got the right answer with the wrong work. He wasn't going to try to find a way for me to pass the BASS test. Perfect Phil was going to get *perfectly* even. Which was going to make me . . .

Perfectly doomed.

'Let's go to my office,' said Dr Daniels.

I thought, Just this once, could we ALL forget about the past?

CHAPTER 30

'I know the work Nick showed doesn't lead to the correct answer,' said Dr Daniels, sitting across from me at her desk.

Perfect Phil nodded perfectly as he stood at the door next to Mr Wickler.

I said, 'But I put down the right answer. It was the answer in my HEAD!'

Perfect Phil folded his perfect arms and looked perfectly serious.

'I didn't cheat!' I said.

'I'm Nick's maths teacher,' said Mr Wickler. 'And I was the examiner for his BASS test. Nick can be stubborn and difficult and more than a little annoying, but he didn't and doesn't cheat.'

Dr Daniels added, 'In fact, he's never been accused of cheating.'

Whoa. I was going to have to rethink my whole Adults' Heads Are Filled with Cheese Dust Theory.

Perfect Phil nodded slowly.

Mr Wickler continued, 'This is a bright, capable kid who just doesn't happen to fit in to some sort of tidy standardised world.'

Dr Daniels stood up. 'Nick has a visual-spatial learning disorder. His brain doesn't work like yours and mine. Does it really matter *how* he got the right answer as long as he *got* it?'

Perfect Phil looked at Dr Daniels, then at Mr Wickler, then at me. Then Perfect Phil flashed his perfect smile. 'Thank you for your time, everyone.'

Perfect Phil said, 'I'll get back to you with a decision—'

Everyone's phones went off at once. Dr Daniels said, 'We have a situation with the Schoolseum.'

SOMETHING ABOUT A MONKEY AND A VOLCANO.

BOB?

CHAPTER 31

I said to Memaw, 'Where's Bob?'

She said, 'One second he was checking my scalp for fleas, and the next . . . '

Bob was sitting on top of Maria Olmera's 1/3,000 scale model of Krakatoa – a volcano whose eruption in 1883 was heard three thousand miles away.

'Did you bring his monkey treats?' I said.

Memaw patted her purse. 'Right here.'

I said, 'Good. Use them to try to get him down.'

Molly, Becky, Simone and Karl walked up. Molly said, 'Is this part of your plan?'

Is it?

I searched the room. I saw Molly's potato-powered mobile phone charger and Karl's Stanley-powered toothbrush, and then finally, what I was looking for. . . .

'That's MY Taj Mahal,' I said. 'She stole my idea. Are you kidding me?'

'What?' said Molly.

'Never mind,' I said. 'Yes, of course this is all part of my plan. Now—'

Molly interrupted. 'Before we hear your plan, Karl has something to say.'

Karl cleared his throat. 'It's wrong to trick your friends into thinking their pet sea monkeys can sing "Frère Jacques".'

I said, 'You're right. I'm sorry, Karl.'

'You can make it up to me,' said Karl, 'by coming over for a playdate where we can sing it together.'

I said, 'Only little kids have playdates, Karl.'

'DO IT!' said Molly, Becky and Simone all at once.

'Every Saturday for two months,' said Karl.

'Fine,' I said. 'Now here's my plan.'

Karl raised his hand.

I said, 'Yes, Karl.'

'The Beret-Cam can't record directly to a flash drive.'

'I know that and you know that, but Alice doesn't know that.'

'Ohhhhhhh,' said Karl.

'Bob wanna treat?' said Memaw as she held out

her hand at the base of the volcano. Bob jumped down, grabbed the treat, and then scampered right back to the top.

I said, 'We need to do this now, while everyone is distracted.'

We all started walking toward Alice. I said, 'Yup, that was us!'

'You mean it was you who let the python out of the cage during the science fair?' said Becky.

'We rigged the cage to open remotely. Isn't that right, Molly?'

'Yes, Nick, that's RIGHT! And don't forget all those chalk drawings we did on the sidewalks,' said Molly.

Simone said, 'YOU did all those? I mean,

except for the one I did.'

Karl raised his hand again.

I said, 'Karl, you don't have to raise your hand.'

'What about that time milk shot out of my nose at lunch and everybody laughed?' asked Karl. 'Did you do that, too?'

I whispered, 'That wasn't us.' Then louder: 'But we did send you that invitation to join MLEZ, RIGHT?'

'Oh, sorry,' Karl whispered. Then louder: 'That was YOU?'

'YES!' I said. 'THAT was—'

'US!' yelled Alice. 'NOT YOU! US!'

Alice turned beet red. So red, you could really see her. Dr Daniels was right. She should wear more colour.

'You're LYING!' said Alice. 'You didn't do anything! I did EVERYTHING!'

I said, 'You?'

'I mean WE! We did everything! We cleared the way, we ran interference, and we crawled around in dirty air ducts ripping up our favourite pairs of jeans! We didn't take any credit, no one fed us scones, and no one ever invited us over to play Twister with their sea monkeys! NOT ONCE!'

Alice glared at me. 'I know what you're doing. You're trying to get me to confess. But no one's

going to believe you. Because no one believes a sweet, shy, really-hard-to-see girl like *me* could do ANY of that.'

On the other side of the room Memaw begged, 'Please, Bob. Please come to Memaw, Bob.'

'They may not believe us,' I said as I reached under Karl's beret, 'but they'll believe this flash drive that just recorded everything you said with Karl's Beret-Cam.'

Alice stared at the flash drive. 'That's not possible.'

I smiled. 'It's all ov—'

'That's the last treat, Bob!' yelled Memaw. 'I've had it! Get down NOW!'

That's when I learned that, from a distance, a flash drive looks a lot like a monkey treat.

'Now what?' said Molly.

Mr Dupree marched up to the Krakatoa display and said, 'I know how to get him down.'

He nodded to Maria. Maria nodded back.

Then . . .

Karl and I were the first to dig out from under the pile of potatoes, sunflower seeds and volcano guts.

Karl pointed. 'Stanley's flying out the window.'

I looked at Karl. Karl looked at me.

CHAPTER 32

'Come on, Stanley!' pleaded Karl.

She was holding a bag of sunflower seeds from her . . . her . . . MY Taj Mahal.

'No!' yelled Karl. 'They give Stanley gas!'

Alice didn't listen. She threw a handful of sunflower seeds at Stanley. They landed short. She tried again. And again. And again.

'Ignore her, Stanley,' said Karl. 'I've got fresh lemon bars at home.'

I said, 'Boost me up and I'll grab him.'

'Be careful,' said Karl. 'Stanley bites when he's feeling anxious.'

'Terrific.'

I stepped into Karl's cupped hands. I pulled myself up just as a few seeds landed between me and the rocket. I picked one up and looked at Stanley.

Stanley would have to drop the flash drive to take the seed. When he did, I'd grab the drive.

The easiest Kapezki.

WHAM! BL-BLAM! BLAM! TH-THUNK

I pushed Karl off me, expecting to see Alice long gone. But she was standing just a few yards away, staring at Molly, Simone, and Becky running toward her.

'Stop her!' I yelled. 'She's got the flash drive!'

Alice turned to run in the opposite direction. But her path was blocked that way too.

There was only one place for her to go . . .

Alice sprinted toward the storm sewer and
disappeared inside just as Molly, Simone and
Becky arrived.

Molly said, 'What happened?'

Karl stared at Stanley eating sunflower seeds
on the ground. 'You're sleeping alone tonight.'

Molly turned to the storm sewer. 'I'm not going
in there.'

I leaned down and petted Arnold. 'Arnold and I
will get her. Won't we, boy?'

I swear Arnold looked like he shrugged.

'You can't go in there by yourself,' said Becky.

'This is my mess,' I said. 'I'll clean it up. Besides, you guys need to get back to the Schoolseum and stall for me. I need time to deal with Alice, and I don't need Mr Dupree or Dr Daniels looking for me.'

'You sure?' said Molly.

'I'll be fine. C'mon, it's not like I'm going in there after her. I can talk her out.'

They took off back towards the school.

I looked at Arnold as he licked my hand. If only he were scarier. I looked at Rat Cave. If only it were less scary.

I had no idea how I was going to talk Alice out, but then the answer suddenly hit me.

In the face. A drop of water hit me in the face. Then another. Then another and another.

Alice wasn't in Rat Cave anymore. She was in a storm sewer that was soon going to be a RIVER! She needed to get out of there. NOW!

I splashed toward the entrance and past an upturned shopping cart as puddles started to form.

No response. I tried again. 'ALICE! CAN YOU—'

'GO AWAY!' yelled Alice.

I yelled, 'It's raining! It's not safe in there!'

'You're lying!' said Alice.

I looked down. The puddles were merging into a small stream. 'Alice, I'm seriously not lying!'

Alice cried, 'I'm not coming out!'

I looked down again. The water had risen to cover the bottom of the storm drain. I yelled, 'LOOK DOWN AT YOUR FEET, ALICE!'

Nothing.

We were out of time. I had to call for help. I reached for my phone.

'I'm coming out!' yelled Alice.

Thank goodness.

'Ah!' cried Alice. 'My foot! It's stuck!'

I waded in after her. Arnold followed. I stopped. 'Arnold, STAY!'

Arnold barked and suddenly he didn't look like a drowned rat; he looked like that dog Jack from Memaw's show – the one who's always saving Brandon from abandoned clothes dryers.

JACK THE WONDER DOG

ARNOLD THE WET DOG

It was raining. I was squinting.

I thought, Hmm . . . maybe . . .

Arnold's ears pinned back. He barked. Then he took off!

'HELP!' yelled Alice.

I waded in after her. The water was now up to my shins and flowing fast. With just the dim light from the entrance I couldn't see very far. What I could see was a mess of rubbish, cracked concrete, exposed rusting metal bars – and about fifteen feet in – Alice.

She looked scared.

I put my hands in the water and found her foot stuck in a crack in the ground.

Alice grabbed the bar with one hand.

I said, 'Both hands!'

Alice opened her other hand. Inside was the flash drive.

'Get rid of it!' I shouted.

'So that you can come back and get it and show everyone? No way!'

'There's nothing on it anyway!'

'What?'

'DO IT!'

Alice dropped the drive and grabbed the bar
with both hands.

'On three!' I said. 'One . . . two . . . '

We were off our feet and floating quickly
toward the main storm drain. Ahead was the exit.
And the . . .

We had one chance to grab the cart as we passed or else get carried off down the main channel.

'Hug my neck!' I yelled.

'What? Why?' said Alice.

'JUST DO IT!' I cried.

She threw her arms around my neck. We were closing fast on the cart. Too quickly. I reached out my hand and . . .

We pulled ourselves out of the rushing water and onto the trolley.

'Get on my shoulders and pull yourself out!'

'What about you?'

'I'm okay here,' I lied. 'You can get help!'

She climbed onto my shoulders. I could see the water continuing to rise.

If I could get on my feet, Alice would be high enough. I placed one foot in position. Then the other, and . . .

The last thing I saw as I went under was Alice lifting herself up onto the bank. The current pulled me under. I tumbled and rolled until I finally hit the bottom. I got my feet under me and pushed hard.

I'd travelled about thirty feet from the storm sewer. I threw my arms around, reaching for anything to grab, when all of sudden, there she was. . . .

CHAPTER 33

Mr Dupree watched Doris float out of sight.

'She's gone,' I said.

'But you're not,' said Mr. Dupree. 'I'll make that trade any day.'

'Why did you even bring her?' I asked.

'When Molly told me Alice was in the storm sewer, and it started to rain, I grabbed Doris and some towels.'

'Wait. Molly? She was supposed to stall. What about Arnold?'

'Who's Arnold?'

'Never mind.'

'At the end of the day it's just a plunger, Nick. And besides, I still have the other one.'

'Other one?'

'The one you and everyone in Safety Patrol signed? The one you had Alice give me?'

Alice? What?

Mr Dupree said, 'What I don't understand is why you made up that whole Emily story instead of telling me you took Doris so you could make sure you found one just like her.'

'Um . . . we wanted to surprise you?'

Mr Dupree looked at me.

I said, 'Were you surprised?'

Mr Dupree pointed behind me. 'I think someone wants to thank you.'

I turned around.

Alice said, 'Thanks . . . um . . . for, you know . . . '

'Yeah,' I said. 'I just . . . you know, did . . . you know, what—'

Alice smiled. 'I know.'

Then we did that awkward stare-at-your-shoes thing for a few seconds.

Finally I said, 'You gave Mr Dupree the other plunger and signed it from all of us?'

'Yeah. I didn't want you to get in trouble for something I did.'

'But why not tell me that? Why go after the flash drive?'

'I was going to tell you, but then you were taking all the credit for everything I'd done and then you tried to trick me and then I wasn't sure you wouldn't expose me anyway.'

'*You'd* done? Expose *you*?'

Alice took a deep breath. 'MLEZ is me. Just me. There was no Ethel. I started it. I just took the Emily who kids invented years ago to explain stuff they can't explain and made it into MLEZ. Now I'm going to end it.'

'End it?'

'No boy is worth almost drowning for.'

'Boy? Wait. Karl?'

Alice blushed. Sort of. It was hard to tell.

I shook my head. 'KARL?'

Alice smiled. 'The boy has skills.'

I said, 'So it was always about Karl.'

'You heard him in the bathroom. He wants to be up on Humpty Dumpty's wall. And he should be up there. Because he's special.'

'Yeah. I saw you and the others deciding to talk Karl out of MLEZ. I recorded it on my phone.'

'Recorded it?'

'But I deleted it. I could never use it. It would have hurt Karl too much. He really likes all of you. I mean, he really, *really* likes all of you. And now I know why.'

'Um . . . why?'

'The . . . whole . . . you know, almost-drowning thing?'

'Oh. That.'

It was a lot to take in. An invisible girl starts a super-secret club because she wants to give a weird kid a chance to be up on a wall. Then the weird kid's friends butt in and the invisible girl almost drowns and now the weird kid will . . .

Alice said, 'We should probably get back to the Schoolseum.'

'Wait,' I said. 'Karl deserves better.'

'What are you saying?'

'I'm pretty good at doing the wrong thing for the right reasons. And you're good at doing the right thing for – well, really weird reasons. Together maybe we could try doing the right thing for the right reasons.'

'Keep MLEZ going?' asked Alice.

'Why not? We help Karl get up on that wall. You get to be, you know, near Karl. We all get to help the school. It's win-win- . . . win? Wait. I lost track of wins.'

'A lot of wins.'

'So?'

Alice nodded. 'Let's do it.'

We shook hands then started back toward the school.

SERIOUSLY, KARL?   SERIOUSLY.

CHAPTER 34

Alice and I returned to the Schoolseum to a lot of awkward hugging and to hear Perfect Phil's decision on my BASS test score. Which didn't happen right away because Perfect Phil had to torture me first by delaying his decision until after the Schoolseum. Apparently he's into spud power.

... and cutting-edge tooth-brushing technology ...

. . . and uncooperative mythological mischief-makers.

Finally I watched as Dr Daniels grabbed Perfect Phil and motioned me to join them in the hall. But Perfect Phil shook his head, then grabbed a chair and climbed up. Great. It wasn't enough to find out I've disappointed everyone; I have to find out *in front* of everyone.

'Quiet!' yelled Perfect Phil. 'Earlier today I met with a student who took the BASS test and failed to show his work. Showing your work is important. If we can't see your work, we educators can't know if you understand what we're teaching.'

Unless you understand perfectly and don't need to show your work to get the right answer, I thought.

Perfect Phil continued, 'Unless the student does understand and doesn't need to show his or her work to get the right answer.'

Whaaaaaaat?

'Standardised tests are useful,' said Perfect Phil. 'But not when you're testing a nonstandardised student. That kind of student does a lot better on nonstandardised tests. Like this Schoolseum. I see with my own eyes that Nick Ramsey, like the rest of you, can . . .

SHOW YOUR WORK!

'I hereby declare his answer on the show-your-work problem to be correct. Emily Dickinson Middle School is therefore decreed an exemplary-rated school. And I think you all know what that means.'

What just happened?

As everyone celebrated (with Karl celebrating a little more than made everyone comfortable), I looked for Alice. And I found her right away, all bright and shiny and totally easy to see.

'You're like a superhero, Nick,' said Mr Dupree from behind me.

I turned around. Mr Dupree and Memaw were standing together by a window.

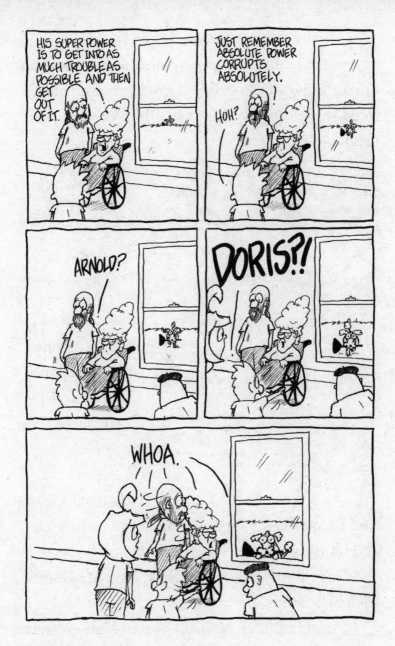

Whoa.

ACKNOWLEDGMENTS

Once again, I'd like to thank my terrific editor, Lisa Yoskowitz, for saying things like 'No.' 'No way. Are you kidding me?' 'Better.' 'Nice.' 'Very good.' 'Awesome.' And just once: 'Super awesome.'

Thank you also to my agent, Dan Lazar, for his advice and counsel, and letting me do that thing I shouldn't have done and later not saying, 'I told you so.'

And a big thank-you to my family and friends for their patient support of the cranky cave-dwelling hermit I become when I'm writing/drawing on deadline.

When you start one of these things, you have no idea how you're going to get to the end. Yet somehow you do. It's always a struggle. But a struggle made easier by the dedicated support of agents, editors, designers, copy editors, production people, marketers, salespeople, publicists, family and friends.

In Texas we have a saying: *You dance with who brung you*. I hope I can continue to dance with all of you for a long time.

MICHAEL FRY

spent middle school as a geeky, nerdy Chess Club member who played the French horn — and loved every minute of it (well, most minutes).

His school days behind him, Mike is the author of the Odd Squad series and the co-creator and writer of several comic strips, including *Over the Hedge*, which is featured in newspapers nationwide and was adapted into the hit animated movie of the same name. In addition to working as a cartoonist, Mike was a co-founder of RingTales, a company that animates print comics for all digital media, and is an active blogger, tweeter, and public speaker, as well as the proud father of two adult daughters.

Originally from Minneapolis, Mike currently lives with his wife in Austin, Texas. Visit him online at www.oddsquadbooks.com.